The
Patchwork Torah

To my friends and community in Safed: may we have many years together reading from and celebrating with the "Patchwork Torah" that inspired this book. And to my parents, husband and daughter for their love and support. – A.O.

For Pancho, Elie, Helyett, Isabelle and Stephen – E.O.

KAR-BEN PUBLISHING
A division of Lerner Publishing Group, Inc.
241 First Avenue North
Minneapolis, MN 55401 U.S.A.
1-800-4-KARBEN

Website address: www.karben.com

Main body text set in Sassoon Sans Regular 14/20.
Typeface provided by Monotype.

Library of Congress Cataloging-in-Publication Data

Ofanansky, Allison.
    The patchwork Torah / by Allison Ofanansky ; illustrated by Elsa Oriol.
       pages   cm
    Summary: David learned from his grandfather to be a sofer, or scribe, and to care for the Torah scrolls that he receives, no matter their condition, until one day he assembles a complete scroll from pieces damaged in the Holocaust, fire, and floods.
    ISBN 978-1-4677-0426-7 (lib. bdg. : alk. paper)
    ISBN 978-1-4677-2434-0 (eBook)
    [1. Torah scrolls—Fiction. 2. Scribes, Jewish—Fiction. 3. Grandfathers—Fiction. 4. Jews—United States—Fiction.] I. Oriol, Elsa, illustrator. II. Title.
PZ7.O31Pat 2014
[E]—dc23   2013002194

Manufactured in the United States of America
1 – CG – 12/31/13

David's grandfather was a *sofer*, a scribe. The rabbi had asked him to write a new Torah for their synagogue, because the letters in the old scroll had started to crack and fade.

David loved to watch as Grandfather dipped his quill pen into the bottle of ink and carefully wrote Hebrew letters on the long sheets of parchment. It had taken him over a year to complete this Torah.

It was Simchat Torah and David was excited, because tonight in the synagogue, everyone would dance with his grandfather's new Torah. David ran ahead, hopping over mud puddles so he wouldn't ruin his shoes. It was wartime, and shoes were expensive and had to last.

The Patchwork Torah

Allison Ofanansky

illustrated by Elsa Oriol

KAR-BEN
PUBLISHING

Grandfather took the new Torah from the ark. It was wrapped in a velvet cover embroidered with silver thread. Next to it was the old scroll in its faded silk cover.

"Will they throw out the old Torah now that you wrote a new one?" David asked.

"A Torah is not something to be thrown away," Grandfather answered. "I'll put it in my cabinet, and someday maybe I'll have time to repair the letters, so it can be used again."

David understood it was important to repair and reuse things. He and his friends went on scrap drives, collecting metal, rubber, and paper to make things that would help the soldiers fighting against Hitler in Europe.

As his grandfather carried the scroll around the synagogue people touched it, then kissed the tips of their fingers. David marched proudly beside him.

Years passed. When he became a Bar Mitzvah, David was called up to read from his grandfather's Torah.

Afterward, Grandfather told David he was now old enough to learn the skills of a sofer. He taught David how to sharpen the quills and how to use them to write Hebrew letters on a scrap of paper.

One day when David was practicing, there was a knock on the door. He and Grandfather hurried to greet their long-awaited guests.

A tall thin man cradled a Torah wrapped in a worn blanket. A small woman stood by his side. Cousins Sarah and Ben had survived the terrible war in Europe and only recently arrived in the United States. They handed their treasure to Grandfather.

During lunch, Sarah and Ben told their story.

"We ran from our house when we heard the Nazi soldiers coming," Ben said. "The synagogue was destroyed. We saw the Torah scroll in a mud puddle and grabbed it and ran. Finally, after hours of searching, we found an old barn to hide in."

"The farmer found us in the morning," Sarah said. "We thought he would turn us in, but he let us stay. The barn was cold in the winter, wet in the spring, and full of flies in the summer. But at least we were safe. The farmer's wife brought us food. We hid the Torah under a pile of hay."

"The scroll got wet," Ben added. "And mice chewed on the parchment. Do you think you can fix it?"

Grandfather unrolled the scroll and studied it. "I am afraid much of it is damaged," he said. He wrapped it back in the blanket and put it in his cabinet. "When I have time someday, I'll see what I can do, but I'm not sure whether it can be used again."

Years passed. When David grew up, he became a sofer like his grandfather. In his workshop stood his grandfather's cabinet of old scrolls. One day, another Torah was added.

David's son, Josh, was watching him work when the rabbi called.

"There was a fire in the synagogue last night," the rabbi said.

"No one was hurt, but the Torah scroll was damaged."

"The one my grandfather wrote?" David asked.

"Yes, I'm afraid so."

"I will come and get it. Maybe it can be repaired."

David unrolled the scroll. Parts of the parchment had been singed by flames or blackened by smoke. He brought it home and put it in the cabinet with the two other scrolls.

"Why do you keep all those old scrolls, Dad?" Josh asked.

David pointed to each of the scrolls and told its story. "This is a very old Torah whose letters have cracked and faded. This one was rescued by my grandfather's cousins, who kept it with them while they hid in a barn during the Holocaust. And the one that was damaged in the fire is one my grandfather wrote. Maybe someday I can fix them all."

Years passed. David taught his grandchildren how to sharpen quills and how to write Hebrew letters on scraps of paper. He hoped one of them would be a sofer someday.

One day as David was working on a new Torah, his son called from New Orleans. "There was a big flood here, Dad." Josh told him about the hurricane called Katrina, and how the water of the Mississippi River overflowed the levees and poured through the streets and houses.

"Our synagogue flooded, too," Josh said. "I waded in to rescue the Torah, but the water came almost to my waist. I held the Torah as high as I could as I carried it out, but I'm afraid much of it got wet."

"Bring it to me," David said.

When Josh brought the Torah from New Orleans, his daughter Leah came with him. Leah loved to watch Grandpa David work.

David saw how the water had soaked through most of the parchment. He shook his head and opened his cabinet. "I'm getting quite a collection of damaged Torah scrolls," he said to his son and granddaughter. "I had hoped to fix them, but each scroll has parts which just can't be repaired."

"Can you patch them together and make one scroll, Grandpa?" Leah asked. "We just learned about recycling at school. You could make a recycled Torah!"

"What a wonderful idea," David said, smiling at his granddaughter. "I will try to have it done before Simchat Torah."

For the next several months David was very busy.

With a sharp knife, he cut out good parts from each of the damaged Torah scrolls.

He set aside the ruined sections to send to a *genizah*, a special storage place for old holy books.

With sinew and a thick needle, he patched together the pieces of parchment which were not damaged.

With his quill pen, he replaced missing letters and darkened faded words.

It was hard work, but it made him happy.

On Simchat Torah, David's children and grandchildren joined him at the synagogue to honor the new Torah. When the singing and dancing were over, everyone took seats and David carried the scroll to the bima. He opened it, recited the blessings, and read the final words of the Torah from the new scroll.

Then he and the rabbi began to roll it back to the beginning.

"This is a very unusual scroll," David told the congregation. "The writing is not the same all the way through. I wrote part of it. Other sofers, in other places and at other times, wrote other parts."

Leah stood on her toes and watched the parchment flow past, as her grandpa pointed out where the sections had been patched together. He told the stories behind each one.

"Now," said the rabbi, "We will begin the cycle of Torah reading once again."

He recited the blessings and read the first lines, "In the beginning..."

When it was time to return the Torah to the ark, David carried it around the synagogue. He remembered the Simchat Torah, so long ago, when he marched with his grandfather. He smiled at Leah. She held her grandpa's hand and walked proudly alongside him.

ALLISON OFANANSKY, born in the United States, now lives in the village of Kaditah, Israel near the mystical city of Safed, with her husband and daughter. They enjoy hiking the hills of the Galilee, gathering and eating the fruits that grow there. They are involved in many environmental and eco-peace projects. Allison is the author of Kar-Ben's *Nature in Israel Holiday Series* that includes *Harvest of Light, Sukkot Treasure Hunt, What's the Buzz: Honey for a Sweet New Year* and *Cheesecake for Shavuot.*

ELSA ORIOL completed her studies in Graphic Arts, Interiors Architecture, and Decorative Painting in France. After working several years as an interiors architect, she is now dedicated to painting and illustration. She works in acrylics and gouache.